...cu-u-use me:

...at's going on?" It was Donald.

Just what I needed!" I muttered to myself.

"Hide and seek?" Donald drawled through the window. He likes to think of himself as years older than Kate, Stephanie, Patti, and me and tons more sophisticated.

I switched off my flashlight. "No," I said. "I've lost something."

"Your mittens," Donald said. I guess he was referring to the nursery rhyme, which I didn't think was very funny at all.

"No," I snapped. "A valuable rhinestone pin!"

Donald stared at me. "Excu-u-use me!" he huffed, slamming the window shut.

I went back to my house and quickly dialed Stephanie's private number.

She answered on the first ring. "Find it?" she asked breathlessly.

"Nope," I said.

"Oh, wow." Stephanie sounded worried. "I hope *Kate* doesn't find it. . . ."

"If she does, we'll know soon enough," I said gloomily.

Look for these and other books
in the Sleepover Friends Series:

1 *Patti's Luck*
2 *Starring Stephanie*
3 *Kate's Surprise*
4 *Patti's New Look*
5 *Lauren's Big Mix-Up*
6 *Kate's Camp-Out*
7 *Stephanie Strikes Back*
8 *Lauren's Treasure*
9 *No More Sleepovers, Patti?*
#10 *Lauren's Sleepover Exchange*
#11 *Stephanie's Family Secret*
#12 *Kate's Sleepover Disaster*
#13 *Patti's Secret Wish*
#14 *Lauren Takes Charge*
#15 *Stephanie's Big Story*
#16 *Kate's Crush*
#17 *Patti Gets Even*
#18 *Stephanie and the Magician*
#19 *The Great Kate*

Super Sleepover Guide

The Great Kate

Susan Saunders

AN
APPLE
PAPERBACK

SCHOLASTIC INC.
New York Toronto London Auckland Sydney

ISBN 0-590-42815-2

12 11 10 9 8 7 6 5 4 3 2 1   9/8 0 1 2 3/9

Printed in the U.S.A.   28

First Scholastic printing, December 1989

The Great Kate

Chapter
1

"I can't believe we're actually sitting here staring at spoons!" Kate Beekman exclaimed. "I feel like an idiot!"

"Oh, come on, Kate!" Stephanie Green said. "You could at least *try*."

"Read that paragraph over again, Lauren," Patti Jenkins said to me — I'm Lauren Hunter. It was a Friday night and the sleepover was at my house that week. The four of us were upstairs in my bedroom, sprawled on the floor around a big pile of munchies: a king-size bag of barbecue potato chips, a bowl of my special onion-soup-olives-bacon-bits-and-sour-cream dip, a can of butterscotch popcorn, and a gallon of Dr Pepper to wash it all down.

"Yeah. Read the part about the white light," Stephanie instructed.

" 'After leading the group through several minutes of deep-breathing relaxation exercises,' " I slowly read the newspaper article, ignoring Kate's groans, " 'Mrs. Keller, the leader, said, "Imagine a hot, white light streaming out of the ceiling, down through your head, into your shoulders, down your arms, etcetera. . . ." ' "

"Etcetera?" Stephanie asked.

"Hands and fingers, I guess," I said.

Kate shot me a long-suffering look.

"Go on," Patti murmured encouragingly.

" ' "Let it pour into the spoons you are holding," Mrs. Keller said. "Feel the heat building . . . building . . . building." ' " I lowered the sheet of newspaper and focused on my own spoon again. I tried to imagine an enormous spotlight aimed straight down at the top of my head. . . .

Stephanie frowned intently at the spoon in her hands. "I think I'm beginning to feel the heat!" she cried excitedly.

"Of course you are," Kate muttered. "The radiator's on full-blast!"

I started reading quickly, before Stephanie could

2

answer Kate back. Sometimes it doesn't take much for those two to really get going.

" ' "Now let's chant together," Mrs. Keller commanded, "Bend! Bend! Bend!" And one by one, the spoons started bending like Play-Doh!' "

I put the paper down, stared hard at my spoon, and began to chant, "Bend! Bend! Bend!"

Stephanie and Patti joined in, but Kate tossed her spoon onto the floor and rolled her eyes. "This is definitely getting embarrassing!"

"Kate, you're wrecking the mood!" Stephanie complained. Then Stephanie dropped her spoon, too. After a moment, she picked it up again, and stuck it into the bowl of my special dip. She scooped out a spoonful and licked at it thoughtfully. "Kate, you're always saying 'mind over matter,' " she pointed out. "And that is exactly what we're talking about here."

Kate does say "mind over matter" a lot. It's one of her favorite expressions, along with, "You're letting your imagination run away with you again." And usually the word she sticks at the end of both of those sentences is the same: "Lauren."

It's just that Kate is so super-sensible that I look a little flakey by comparison. In fact, it's pretty amazing we're such good friends because we're as different as two people can be. Kate's incredibly neat; I was *born* messy. She's organized; I'm more or less scattered. She's always on time; I'm usually late. She's small and blonde; I'm tall and dark. In fact, maybe we wouldn't get along so well if we hadn't been hanging out together since we were babies.

We're almost next-door neighbors on Pine Street in Riverhurst — there's just one house between us. So, it wasn't surprising that we started playing together when we were still in diapers. By the time we were in kindergarten you couldn't *pry* us apart. That's when the sleepovers started.

Every Friday night, either I would sleep over at Kate's house, or she would sleep over at mine. Soon it was such a regular thing that Kate's dad named us the Sleepover Twins.

In those days, sleepovers meant s'mores in the toaster oven, cherry Kool-Pops in the freezer, and non-stop games of Dress-Up and Let's Pretend. What can you expect from little kids? But as we got older there were major improvements. For one thing, Kate started making her fabulous marshmallow superfudge, and I invented my special dip. For another, we discovered Mad Libs and Truth or Dare. We also put in thousands of hours watching movies on TV. Old, new, black-and-white, color, horrors, musicals — we'd watch them all. Kate's a real movie freak and plans to be a director some day.

For years the Sleepover Friends were just Kate and me. Then, last year, Stephanie Green moved from the city to a house at the other end of Pine Street. She and I got to know each other because we were both in 4A, Mr. Civello's class.

Stephanie told funny stories about her life back in the city. She could do all the latest dance steps, and she had a terrific eye for clothes. I thought she was great! I wanted Kate to get to know her, too. So without making a big thing of it, I invited Stephanie to a sleepover at my house.

Talk about your total disaster! Kate thought Stephanie was an airhead who *only* cared about clothes. Stephanie thought Kate was a stuffy know-it-all. My brother, Roger, said the problem was obvious: "They're too much alike — both bossy!"

Whatever the reasons, it looked as if the two of them were more likely to become enemies-for-life than friends-for-life. But I can be plenty stubborn when I want to, and I decided I wasn't going to give up that easily.

Since all three of us lived on Pine Street, it was only natural that we'd fall into the habit of riding our bikes back and forth to school together. After a few weeks of that, I arranged with Stephanie to meet us at the mall for a Saturday of shopping at Just Juniors.

Then Stephanie invited Kate and me to a sleep-over at her house. Stephanie's mom makes fabulous peanut-butter-chocolate-chip cookies, which Kate loves almost as much as movies. Success! Little by little, the Sleepover Twins became a threesome.

Then Patti Jenkins showed up in Mrs. Mead's fifth-grade class along with Kate and Stephanie and me.

Patti's from the city, too. She and Stephanie even went to the same school there for a couple of years. But they didn't seem to have much more in common. Patti's as quiet and shy as Stephanie is out-going.

Kate and I both liked Patti right away. We quickly found out that she's one of the smartest kids in our class, and one of the nicest. And she's the only girl in fifth grade who's taller than I am. So when Stephanie wanted her to be part of our gang, we thought it was a great idea! School had barely started this fall, before there were *four* Sleepover Friends!

As well as having our sleepovers every Friday,

we spend practically all of our free time together. But that doesn't necessarily mean all four of us always see eye to eye. Like Kate and me: She thinks I should put the brakes on my imagination, and sometimes she's right. I have been known to get just a bit carried away about ghosts and UFO's.

But life would be pretty dull without a little imagination to spice things up, wouldn't it? That's why I didn't think it would hurt Kate to loosen up a little. Even though, by the way she was acting, I had to admit it didn't seem very likely.

Chapter
2

Stephanie must have been thinking along the same lines, because she gripped her spoon tightly with both hands and said, "Kate — we're trying to have some fun here. Bend . . . bend. . . ."

"What this *is*, is *not* fun," Kate replied firmly. "It's a total waste of time." She turned to me. "Where did you get that article, anyway, Lauren?" She grabbed the sheet of newspaper and opened it to look at the front page. "No wonder!" Kate made a face. "One of those awful rags they sell at the supermarket! 'Is Second-Grader Really a One-Hundred-Year-Old Alien?' 'Girl With Two Heads Says Two Are Better Than One.' Lauren, did you pay for this?!"

"No, it was wrapped around a flower pot Mom bought at Hearts and Flowers," I mumbled, staring down at my sneakers.

"I can't think of a better use for it, unless maybe to line a trash can," Kate said. She handed it back to me. "The Quarks Club would laugh their heads off if they could see you reading this, Patti."

The Quarks Club is a science club with some of the smartest kids at Riverhurst Elementary for members. Naturally, Patti belongs. And I expected her to agree with Kate, because even *I* had to admit that what we were doing wasn't exactly scientific. But Patti surprised me — and Kate.

"Mr. Murdock says the most important thing for a scientist to have is an open mind," she answered. Mr. Murdock is one of the teachers in charge of the club. "Actually, we've read about Mrs. Keller, and a man in Italy called the Great Conti, and Maria Vilar, a little girl in South America. . . ."

"All of these people sit around bending spoons?!" Kate broke in. She sounded shocked.

"No," Patti replied. "But all of them are psychics — people who seem to be able to do mysterious things with their minds. And even scientists can't really come up with a good explanation of *how* they

9

do them. Like telling the color of something while they're blindfolded, just by touching it. . . ."

"I can do that," Kate said. Squeezing her eyes shut, she reached out and touched Stephanie's foot. "Hmmm — I feel . . . red . . . black . . . and white!" she said in a hollow voice.

"You're right, O Great Kate!" Stephanie cried. Pretending to be amazed, she pulled up one leg of her sweats so we could see her red-white-and-black checked socks.

Then all of us giggled, because red, white, and black are Stephanie's favorite colors, and she wasn't likely to be wearing any other color.

"You see," Kate said. "Nothing to it. I'll bet all that spoon-bending and the other junk those guys do are just tricks, too."

"Come on, Kate!" Stephanie groaned. "Loosen up!" Those were my thoughts exactly.

"What else do psychics do, Patti?" I asked.

"Oh, they find things that are lost, or beam thoughts to people miles away," Patti answered. "Or else they pick any spot on a map of the world and describe what it looks like there, even if they've never traveled out of their town. Some make plants grow faster — "

"Whoa! Back up a second," Stephanie interrupted. "What's this business about beaming thoughts?"

Patti nodded. "There've been experiments where psychics look at a photograph," she explained, "and beam thoughts about what they see to a person in another city, and that person will be able to describe the photograph in detail! Or a psychic might beam a request for the person to telephone him or her, and — "

"All ri-i-ight!" Stephanie said. "That sounds right up our alley! Let's try it."

"Who did you have in mind, Stephanie?" Kate teased. "It couldn't be Kyle Hubbard?" Kyle Hubbard is the boy Stephanie liked *that* week. He's in our class.

"Why not?" Stephanie shrugged. "This psychic stuff could be better than Truth or Dare. We won't have to call the guys — we'll make them call us! How is it supposed to work, Patti?"

"Okay," Patti said. "First you have to think of Kyle really hard. Then, when you're got a clear picture of him, try to imagine where he is *right* now."

"It's ten-thirty-five. He's probably at home," Stephanie said.

"Watching *Friday Chillers*," Kate added. She knows Kyle pretty well because they were in the same class last year, and Kyle's as much of a movie freak as she is. "That's what we would be doing, too, if we had any sense."

"Now, when you've got a picture of Kyle in your minds," Patti went on, "close your eyes and imagine him sitting in front of a TV set, watching *Friday Chillers*." Patti paused. "Think really hard: Kyle, call Lauren's house. Kyle, call Lauren's house. . . ."

I closed my eyes and tried to picture Kyle. He's shorter than I am, and stocky, with brown curly hair and big brown eyes. He'd worn a light-blue shirt to school that day, and jeans, so I imagined him still wearing them. I shut my eyes tighter. Kyle was sitting on the floor in a dark room, really close to a TV set. The light from the screen was flickering across his face. . . .

"Kyle, call Lauren's house. Kyle, call Lauren's house," I repeated slowly to myself. I imagined my thoughts floating through the roof up into the sky, moving across Riverhurst, and then sinking through Kyle's roof. . . .

"This is dumb!" Kate exclaimed so loudly that I jumped. "*And* we're out of soda. I'm going down to the kitchen." She scrambled to her feet.

"Ka-ate!" Stephanie groaned. "Try to have an open mind, for a change."

"My mind is fine, thank you very much!" Kate pushed my bedroom door open a crack and peered down the dark hall toward my parents' bedroom. "It's just that some people around here have minds that are so open, they're as full of holes as Swiss cheese! Come on! Let's go get that soda." She held her finger to her lips and tiptoed out into the hall. Stephanie, Patti, and I followed her, although I, for one, was feeling pretty cranky about it.

"If we all don't have the right attitude, this psychic stuff doesn't have a chance of working!" Stephanie whispered as we headed for the stairs.

"It doesn't have a chance of working anyway!" Kate hissed back. "It's all faked. Just a bunch of grown-up fairy tales!"

"Kate, you can't always have the answer for everything!" Stephanie muttered. "In fact . . ."

This was an argument that could go on all night, but at that point, we stepped into the kitchen and I turned on the overhead light.

"Wow! What an enormous spider plant!" Patti said enthusiastically. Patti is great at changing the subject whenever there's an argument brewing.

"Yeah," I agreed. "This is the plant Mom bought the new pot for at Hearts and Flowers. It had totally outgrown its old one," I went on. "She must have repotted it today."

The spider plant was sitting on the kitchen counter next to the sink. Spider plants are the ones that look sort of like clumps of grass. They have long, thin leaves, striped light-green and white. At the end of their pale stems, they grow baby spider plants. And as long as you don't forget to water them or something, they'll just keep growing and growing. My mom's plant is huge, about the size of a bushel basket, with tons of babies.

Patti studied it thoughtfully.

"Hey, we could try a psychic experiment of our own, if you guys want to," she said.

"Oh, yeah? What?" Stephanie asked.

"Remember how I said some psychics claim they can make plants grow faster?" Patti pointed to the little baby spider plants. "We could pot eight of these — two for each of us. Then every day we could beam good thoughts to one of them and not the other. At the end of a couple of weeks, we could measure

14

them to see if our thoughts made any difference in their growth.''

I was amazed. I would never have come up with a plan like that. Anyone could see why Patti was a member of the Quarks Club. But Kate wasn't impressed at all.

"Staring at plants is only a little less goofy than staring at spoons,'' she grumped.

"Afraid you're going to be proven wrong, Kate?'' Stephanie said. I could tell she was getting pretty fed-up with Kate's attitude.

"Get real!'' Kate said with a superior sigh.

"Then why don't we try it!'' Stephanie said.

Suddenly, the wall phone rang!

Chapter
3

For a moment we were all too startled to do anything. Then Stephanie giggled. "Maybe you've already been proven wrong, Kate!" she squealed.

"No way that's Kyle," Kate said as the phone rang again.

"I don't care who it is!" I yelped. "Grab it!"

Stephanie was closest to the phone. Just as she threw herself across the kitchen table, Roger burst through the far door — his bedroom is downstairs next to the den. Stephanie still managed to snag the phone first.

"Hello?" she said breathlessly. Then her face fell. "Oh . . . sure. It's for you, Roger."

Roger grabbed the phone. Then he scowled at

the four of us. "Could I have a little privacy around here?" he growled.

"Sure. We just came down for more soda." I pulled a bottle out of the fridge. "Come on, you guys," I said.

The four of us strolled out into the hall, just far enough so that Roger couldn't see us from where he was standing. Then we stopped dead in our tracks to listen.

"Hello," Roger said.

There was a long silence while the other person talked.

"Yeah. Did you see her?"

"Her?" Stephanie mouthed at me.

"Linda," I whispered back. Linda Breslin is, or rather *was*, Roger's girlfriend.

"You saw her at Ekhart's?" Roger squawked. "Who was she with?"

Ekhart's is an ice-skating rink where a lot of the high school kids hang out on weekends.

"Al Frances?! You're kidding me! . . . Oh, yeah?" Roger thundered. "If she'd rather go out with that jerk than with me. . . . Yeah. Those are the breaks," Roger said in a lower voice. ". . . No way I'm apologizing. . . . Yeah," He sighed loudly.

17

"Thanks, Scott." Scott Rudin's one of the guys on the high school track team with Roger. "Catch you tomorrow."

The four of us streaked down the hall and were halfway up the stairs before Roger had hung up the phone.

As soon as we got to my room and closed the door behind us, Stephanie said, "So Roger and Linda *still* aren't speaking."

I shook my head.

"How long has it been?" Kate asked.

"Five days," I replied. I opened the bottle of Dr Pepper and poured some in everyone's glass. "And Roger has been getting grouchier and grouchier. He almost bit my head off this morning just because I used his knife to spread jam on my English muffin."

"Who's Al Frances?" Patti wondered.

"He's a senior," Kate said. Roger's only a junior. "You've seen him," she went on. "He works at the Burger Joint on Saturdays. Light brown hair, cut really short, and lots of muscles."

"He's on the student council this year," I said. "Definitely a hunk."

"I think Roger's cuter," Stephanie said loyally.

"Really?" I stared at her in surprise. It's hard for me to think of Roger as anything other than my brother, but I *guess* he is cute. He's tall, like everyone else in my family, with reddish-brown hair and a squarish face like my dad's. When he's in a good mood, his eyes are a nice blue-green. When he's in a bad mood, though, they look much darker. And they'd been looking pretty dark since the weekend before.

"How did all this get started?" Stephanie asked. I could tell she was dying to know everything.

"I'm not sure of the gruesome details," I said. "Roger's not going to tell *me* anything. But from what I've overheard, it seems that Roger forgot their sixth anniversary. . . ."

"They've been going steady for six years?!" Patti squeaked. She looked flabbergasted.

"No," Kate said, giggling. "Six months."

"Anyway, Roger forgot all about it," I went on. "And I guess Linda got mad. Then Roger got mad, too. Then Linda said she didn't want to go steady anymore. So she gave Roger back his track sweater. Now she's waiting for him to apologize. . . ."

"And he won't," Patti said, nodding.

"Right. You heard him," I said. "And pretty soon he's going to be so impossible that Mom and Dad and I will have to move out!"

Roger's usually a pretty good brother. We jog together two or three times a week. He lets me borrow his typewriter for homework papers, and sometimes on weekends, he even drives Kate, Stephanie, Patti, and me places. But that weekend Roger was about as easy to get along with as your average grizzly bear!

Luckily, Mom and Dad had lent me their new portable TV for the night. So we didn't have to worry about running into Roger again on our way to the TV in the den. Instead, we holed up in my bedroom and tuned in to *Friday Chillers* on Channel 24. We were just in time to catch the opening credits of the second movie: *The Alien Pods Conquer Manhattan*.

"They look like big spoons!" Stephanie exclaimed as the leader of the alien pods lurched across the screen.

"Don't start with spoons, Stephanie," Kate warned.

And that was as close as we got to psychics for the rest of the evening.

* * *

20

But if Kate thought Stephanie would drop the psychic business without a struggle, she was wrong. While we were eating breakfast the next morning, Stephanie raised her eyebrows at me. "Don't forget to ask your mom about the spider plants, Lauren," she said.

"Huh?" I said. I was busy concentrating on my mom's great whole wheat pancakes with fresh strawberries. "Oh — sure." I put down my fork. "Hey, Mom. Could we clip some of the babies off your spider plant?" I called into the living room.

"Be my guest," my mom called back. "There are little clay pots and potting soil in the basement if you need them."

Kate looked at Stephanie and me disapprovingly. "You know this is pointless," she said sternly.

"You're entitled to your opinion, Kate," Stephanie replied breezily, "even though I for one, think you couldn't be more wrong."

While Kate watched from the kitchen table, Patti, Stephanie, and I picked out eight more or less identical little spider plants. They were all around two and a half inches tall — Patti measured them. We stuck them into clay pots, poured some dirt around them, and gently packed it down.

"All set!" Stephanie said.

She lined the little spider plants up along the kitchen counter. Then Patti took a red marker and wrote A on four of them and B on the other four. She handed each of us one A pot and one B pot. "We'll water them the same amount," she said, "and give them the same amount of light. The only difference will be the psychic difference! All of us have to give plant A all of the good feelings we can come up with. You know, we have to beam it warmth and nice thoughts and encourage it to — "

"I know, I know!" Kate groaned, rolling her eyes. "Grow, grow, grow!"

That afternoon Patti had a Quarks meeting. Kate was going to visit her great-aunt Lela with her sister, Melissa, and their mom. Aunt Lela lives in Medford, which is about thirty miles from Riverhurst. Stephanie said she'd promised to stay home and stay with the twins. She has a new baby brother and sister, and they're starting to get interesting.

So my mom drove all three of them home — even Kate, because Stephanie was afraid that if Kate walked home, her plants might catch cold and ruin the experiment.

A couple of hours later, I was upstairs in my room, looking at the latest issue of *Teen Topics*. I was reading all about the "Teen Dream of the Month" who was Kerry Bordeu, the cute older son on *What a Family!* on Channel 6 on Wednesdays — when the telephone rang.

I didn't pay any attention until Roger hollered up the stairs. "Lauren — it's for you. But don't make a career of it. I need the phone!" I sighed. Clearly, Roger's mood hadn't improved at all.

I picked the phone up in the upstairs hall. "Hello?"

"It's Stephanie," she said. "Can you meet me at the mall around one this afternoon? I've got this totally fantastic idea."

Chapter 4

Stephanie was waiting for me at Sweet Stuff, which is definitely the best candy store in Riverhurst. I got there a little late because I had to pump up my bike tire first. When I arrived, Stephanie had already bought a big bag of chocolate-covered almonds, her absolute favorites.

"Have some," she said, handing the bag to me as we headed up the main aisle of the mall.

"Where are we going?" I asked, munching on a couple of the chocolate almonds. "And aren't you supposed to be at home with the twins?"

"I just said that about the twins to throw Kate off the track," Stephanie replied.

"Kate?" I said. "What does your totally fantastic idea have to do with Kate?"

Stephanie smiled mysteriously. "Wait till we get to Hearts and Flowers," she said, "and I make sure they have what I need. Then you'll see. . . ."

And she refused to say another word until we'd pushed open the glass door of Hearts and Flowers and stepped inside.

Being inside Hearts and Flowers is kind of how I imagine a tropical jungle. It's really hot and damp, and there are hundreds of different kinds of plants pressing against you on all sides. They've all got water dripping from their leaves, and there's hardly any room to move. We threaded our way down the narrow trail leading to the counter in the back where the owner, Mrs. Talley, sits.

Mrs. Talley peered at us from behind a big multicolored flower arrangement she was working on. "Hello, girls," she said. "What can I do for you today?"

"I'm looking for a spider plant," Stephanie said.

"Wha-a-a. . . ," I began. I shot Stephanie a look that said: Don't we have *enough* spider plants?!

But Stephanie just poked me with her elbow.

"A smallish one," she said, smiling at Mrs. Talley.

"I have quite a few spider plants against the wall on the left," Mrs. Talley told us. "Why don't you girls take a look, see if there's one you like?"

Mrs. Talley wasn't kidding about quite a few. There must have been at least thirty spider plants, in all sizes from two inches to two or three feet tall.

"Excellent!" Stephanie murmured. She picked one up. "What do you think, Lauren? Doesn't it look about twice as big as ours?" Then she actually pulled a tape measure out of her pocket and held it up to the plant. "Yep," she said with a satisfied smile. "A little over three-and-a-half inches. This plant ought to do it!"

"Stephanie, just what are you up to?" I asked impatiently.

"Shhh," Stephanie put her finger to her lips. "Well," she whispered, "Kate's been getting awfully pushy and so sure about everything lately, don't you think? Maybe a little shaking up wouldn't hurt."

"What kind of shaking up?" I said, still not catching on.

"Like suddenly her plant A, the one she's beaming all those good thoughts to, grows an inch or so practically overnight." Stephanie grinned. Then she held up the three-and-a-half inch spider plant. "*Voila!*"

"Stephanie!" I gasped. Then I giggled. It would be kind of funny! How would Kate ever explain her own psychic powers away?

"That's brilliant!" I whispered.

Stephanie nodded. "I thought you'd be interested."

"But how would we do it? How can we exchange this plant for Kate's plant A without her knowing about it?" I asked.

"First we repot this plant into one of your mom's clay pots at your house," Stephanie began. "We write an A on it with the red marker. Then we pick an afternoon when Kate's not around after school, do a quick change, and shazzam! Kate's psychic powers appear for all to see!" It was clear she'd really given this plan her full attention!

"Well . . . on Tuesdays Kate has the Video Club," I pointed out.

"Perfect," Stephanie said.

27

"But what about Mrs. Beekman and Melissa?" I said.

"I don't think we should tell them," Stephanie said. "The fewer people who know a secret, the easier it is to keep. But if they do find out, Mrs. Beekman has a good sense of humor. And we can bribe Melissa if we have to."

"It might just work," I said.

"Then you're with me on this?" Stephanie asked.

I hesitated. Then I giggled again. Just once, it would be nice if Kate *didn't* have all the answers. "Count me in," I said.

"Great!" Stephanie said. "Maybe we shouldn't tell Patti, either. She might worry about whether or not it would hurt Kate's feelings."

"It definitely won't hurt her feelings," I said. "It might make her furious at first, but then she'll admit that it's exactly the kind of joke she'd play on somebody who needed to learn a lesson."

Stephanie nodded. Then she picked up the spider plant and headed for the counter.

"How much is this one, Mrs. Talley?" she asked.

28

"A dollar ninety-five," Mrs. Talley said. "A good price for such a nice, healthy plant." She picked up a sheet of newspaper — a page from the very same paper that had started it all — and wrapped it around the pot. She handed the plant to me while Stephanie took out her money.

"UFO Fleet Lands in Wisconsin," I read on the side of the plant. Then I stopped myself. Mrs. Talley's paper had already made life complicated enough!

"Did you ride your bike?" I asked Stephanie as we left the store.

"No. Mom dropped me off," Stephanie said. "She's having her hair done at Cut-Ups while Dad stays with the babies." Cut-Ups is two parking lots over from the main mall.

Stephanie checked her watch. "I've got thirty minutes to kill before I'm supposed to meet her there," Stephanie said. "Want to go to the Burger Joint and get some take-out fries?" She raised her eyebrows at me.

What Stephanie meant was, do you want to check out Al Frances, Roger's competition? "Why not?" I said.

We spotted Al as soon as we walked into the

29

Burger Joint. It wasn't hard to pick him out. He works behind the big griddle right at the front of the restaurant. There he was in a white T-shirt and a white apron. He was frying eggs on one corner of the griddle, burgers on another, sausages on another, and talking to three girls from Riverhurst High, *all* at the same time.

"Definitely cool," Stephanie murmured to me. "Two orders of French fries, to go," she said to the man at the cash register.

"Two fries!" the man yelled to Al Frances. Al nodded and lifted a big wire basket of French fries out of a kettle of boiling oil. He shook the fries into two little bags and quickly salted them without ever taking his eyes away from the girls.

He was smooth all right, *very* smooth.

We paid the man at the register, squirted ketchup all over the fries, and sat down on a bench outside the Burger Joint to eat them.

Through the long window across the front of the Burger Joint we watched Al carefully. He was busy flipping pancakes, like Frisbees, onto plates, turning burgers over neatly with one flick of his wrist, and the whole time he kept talking to the girls.

"Excellent moves," Stephanie said.

"And a senior," I added. If Al Frances focused all that charm on Linda . . . . "Poor Roger."

I like Linda a lot. She's cute — small, with long, wavy, dark-brown hair, green eyes, a great smile, and she's really nice, too. "Nothing like Janet Ahrens," I said out loud. Janet was Roger's girlfriend before Linda. I can't stand her. She's really snobby and conceited and was always giving Roger a hard time.

"The worst," Stephanie agreed. "Linda is terrific. It's really too bad. I wish there was something we could do."

"Maybe there is," I said slowly. "Have you read this month's *Teen Topics*? There's an article in it called — "

" 'Twenty Ways to Say You're Sorry Without Crawling,' " Stephanie cut in. "I read that, all right. But somehow I don't think Roger's in the mood to say 'Sorry.' "

"No," I agreed. "But we could do it for him! What if we sent Linda a single red rose from Hearts and Flowers, and just signed the card 'R'?"

"That's perfect!" Stephanie said excitedly,

31

jumping up off the bench. "It'll knock Linda's socks off! She'll think Roger's fabulously romantic!"

And the two of us rushed across the mall to Hearts and Flowers for the *second* time that afternoon.

Chapter
5

I don't know whether or not the rose knocked Linda's socks off, but having it delivered certainly put a major hole in my savings. Anyway, it didn't make Linda call Roger, and he moped around the house all day Sunday, getting grouchier by the minute.

"I can't take it!" I told Kate and Patti on Monday morning. We were waiting on the corner of Pine Street and Hillcrest for Stephanie, so we could all bike to school together.

"If he's not stamping around or griping about something totally *ridiculous*, he's locked in his room with his headphones on, listening to Heat" — that's Roger and Linda's favorite rock band. "And he's acting like a *zombie*. It's getting really depressing."

"Well, if there are twenty ways to say 'sorry' listed in the article, you've still got nineteen more to go," Kate pointed out as Stephanie rolled up on her bike.

Stephanie's eyes met mine. I gave my head a little shake, to let her know that while I'd told Kate and Patti about sending the rose, naturally I hadn't said *anything* about buying a spider plant at Hearts and Flowers. Stephanie let out a long breath.

"Great pin," I said quickly, meaning the rhinestone lightnting bolt Stephanie was wearing on the lapel of her red down jacket. I didn't want Kate or Patti to notice anything was up.

"Thanks. It's my mom's," Stephanie replied. The four of us started pedaling down Hillcrest.

"What about sending Linda candy?" Patti said to me as we came to the stop light.

"Yeah," Kate said. "A pound of chocolate-covered cherries from Sweet Stuff should do the trick."

I sighed. "I don't think I can afford it," I said. "That single red rose just about bankrupted me!"

"I can lend you a couple of dollars," Stephanie said.

"So can I," Patti chimed in.

"Me, too," Kate told me.

"Thanks, but I don't have time to go to the mall this afternoon, anyway," I said. "I promised Mom I'd do the laundry." My mom's started working again, and I have chores to do after school. "I'm busy tomorrow, too," I added. "It looks like we'll have to think of something else."

"Not necessarily. We could run by Charlie's instead," Kate suggested. "There are boxes of candy in that glass case in front, and it's a lot closer than the mall." Charlie's Soda Fountain is on Main Street, only a couple of blocks from Riverhurst Elementary.

"You wouldn't have to pay to have the candy delivered, either." Patti smiled at me. "I can take it to the Breslins', ring their doorbell, and run." Patti lives on Mill Road, and Linda lives one street over on Columbine.

"All right," I said. "It may be expensive, but it's worth it. I don't know about Roger, but *I* personally can't take this break-up much longer."

We turned in at the bike rack in front of the

school. Some of the guys were hanging out by the steps. There was Mark Freedman from our class, Henry Larkin, and Kyle Hubbard.

"Hey!" Kyle called out as soon as he saw us. He strolled in our direction.

"He's probably just now picking up those signals we beamed him on Friday," Kate said with a snicker. "Hey, Kyle!"

Actually, it *was* Friday night Kyle wanted to talk about, but the only signals he'd picked up were the TV signals. "Did you catch the double-feature on *Chillers*?" he asked Kate, after grinning hello at the rest of us.

When Stephanie, Patti, and I left them, they were deep in a discussion about whether or not the second movie would have been better if the pods had melted instead of exploded.

"We'll just see who has the last laugh this time, O Great Kate," Stephanie murmured to me as we walked into the building.

As soon as the final bell rang at three that afternoon, all four of us rode down to Main Street and pulled up in front of Charlie's. Charlie's Soda Fountain is a pretty neat-looking place. It's really old-fashioned, with stained-glass windows that have flower designs on them, a black-and-white tile floor, a long, black-marble counter, and tall wooden booths lined up against the wall.

Kate, Stephanie, Patti, and I stopped in front of the glass case just inside the door to check out the candy. There were round boxes of chocolate turtles for four dollars and ninety-five cents and little square boxes of chocolate truffles for three ninety-five. Then there were square boxes of assorted chocolates that had red velvet roses on top. They cost seven ninety-five.

"One of those," Stephanie said, pointing to a big box. "Linda'll be totally impressed."

"Right," Kate agreed. "She'll see the rose and immediately think it's from Roger!"

"It's an awful lot of money for candy," I said slowly.

"I'm sure we have enough among the four of us," Patti said.

"Well. . . ." I couldn't make up my mind. Was patching up Roger's romance really worth it? Maybe a card would do just as well, and it would only cost a dollar.

"While you're trying to decide, why don't we

37

have our regulars?" Stephanie suggested. "We'll drink fast."

"I guess Mom wouldn't mind," I said.

We went to the pay phone in back to call our mothers and tell them we'd be a little late in getting home. Then we sat where we always sit, in the last booth.

We always order the same thing at Charlie's. Kate gets a Coke float with two scoops of vanilla ice-cream. Stephanie gets a chocolate shake. Patti's favorite is a lime freeze, and I always order a banana smoothie.

We'd almost finished with our drinks, when a car pulled up at the curb outside and some high-school kids climbed out. Todd Schwartz, the quarterback of the football team, was there with his on-again-off-again steady, Mary Beth Young. So was Tug Keeler, another football player, and his girlfriend, Barbara Baxter, the head of the cheerleading squad. And right behind them were Al Frances and Linda.

"I don't believe it!" Kate exclaimed.

As we peered through the window, all three couples crossed the street and walked into Riverhurst Stationery. Al Frances held the door open for Linda, and he kept flashing his perfect smile at her the whole time.

Stephanie shook her head.

"Poor Roger," she said.

I had to agree. "Let's buy the candy with the roses on top," I said. "Roger needs all the help he can get, and he needs it fast!"

Patti dropped the box of Charlie's best assorted chocolates off at the Breslins' on her way home. She called me just afterward to tell me she'd done it. But there was no phone call from Linda that evening. The candy hadn't worked, either.

I'd never realized how expensive it could be to say you're sorry without crawling. I almost wished Roger weren't so stubborn, because helping him was turning out to be a disaster, financially speaking. But I didn't have any time to plan Roger's next move anyway, because the next day, Tuesday, Stephanie and I were pulling the Big Switch.

As soon as school was over, Kate went down to the art studio for the Video Club meeting. Meanwhile, Patti left for the university, to help her dad rearrange the bookshelves in his office (both of Patti's parents are history professors). This meant that Stephanie and I had a whole hour-and-a-half, because the Video Club meetings don't end until four-thirty.

We biked to Pine Street as fast as we could. While I hurried into my house, and got together the planting supplies we'd need, Stephanie dashed home for Mrs. Talley's spider plant. She was back in five minutes flat. We quickly turned the plant out of its white plastic pot and stuck it into one of Mom's clay ones. Stephanie wrote a neat "A" on the side of the clay pot with a marker, and we were done.

"Done with the easy part, anyway," I said to Stephanie. She slipped the repotted spider plant into the front of her jacket and zipped it closed. I stared at her doubtfully. "Do you really think it's smart to wear a bright-red jacket when you're trying to be sneaky?" I asked.

"You don't seriously expect me to dress like G.I. Joe or something?" Stephanie answered huffily. "Brown and green look absolutely dismal together!"

We left through the back door of my house. Bullwinkle barked a couple of times as we passed the garage — Bullwinkle's Roger's dog and he always stays in the garage during the day when it's cold out. But he sounded too sleepy to keep barking for too long.

Stephanie and I slipped out the back gate and into the alley. Then we squeezed through the Fosters' hedge. The Fosters own the house between Kate's and mine.

As we crept across their backyard, Stephanie suddenly slowed down. "I wonder if Donald's around," she whispered. Donald Foster's a seventh-grader. He's also just about the most conceited boy in Riverhurst, but Stephanie actually seems to think he's cute!

"No, thank goodness," I said, giving Stephanie one of my "you can't-be serious!" looks. "I happen to know he has basketball practice on Tuesdays. So hurry up!"

We crawled into the hedge between the Fosters' and Kate's house. Then we crouched down and checked out Beekman territory.

"At least Melissa's not playing outside," Stephanie said, peering into the empty yard.

The house looked pretty still and dark, too. "I don't think anyone's home," I said. "Stay here. I'll try the back door."

I darted out of the hedge. Then I dodged around

Kate's old wooden swing, and tiptoed up the back steps.

I was right. The back door was locked. I ran back to the hedge and scrunched in next to Stephanie.

"Now what?" she said.

"Well, since we're not going to break in," I said, "we'll just have to wait until *some*body comes back."

Stephanie and I shifted around in the bushes, trying to get comfortable.

"Ouch!" Stephanie cried. Reaching up she broke off a branch that had gotten tangled in her hair. "This is no fun," she mumbled. "After all this trouble, I hope the first one home isn't *Kate*."

Chapter 6

Both of my feet had fallen asleep and my teeth were starting to chatter when Stephanie nudged me. "I think I hear a car," she said in a low voice.

We held our breaths and listened. "You're right," I said. "It's coming down Pine."

The sound of the motor got louder and louder. It was Mrs. Beekman's blue car, turning into the driveway!

Mrs. Beekman drove up to the garage and stopped. Then she picked her pocketbook up off the front seat, opened the door, and climbed out.

"Now, what should we do?" Stephanie barely whispered in my ear.

"She's been grocery shopping," I murmured. I

could see the grocery bags piled up on the back seat. "I'll go help her carry them inside. While our backs are toward you, you try to sneak into the house."

Mrs. Beekman had taken out her housekeys, and she was unlocking the kitchen door of the house.

"What if she sees me?" Stephanie hissed.

"No problem," I whispered. "You offer to help with the groceries, too."

I waited until Mrs. Beekman had walked back to the car. As she leaned into it to lift out a grocery bag, I burst out of the hedge and walked casually over to her.

"Hi, Mrs. Beekman," I said.

"Oh, hi, Lauren," Mrs. Beekman replied. "Kate's not here. She's at her Video Club meeting."

"Oh, wow!" I cried, smacking my forehead. "How dumb can I get?!" *Don't overdo it*, I warned myself. "I forgot about the club. Please don't tell Kate I was here, Mrs. Beekman, she'll think I've totally lost it!"

"Okay," Mrs. Beekman said, laughing. "Since Melissa's playing at a friend's house, your secret is safe." Melissa is the biggest blabbermouth around.

"Can I help you take in the groceries?" I asked.

"How nice of you!" Mrs. Beekman said. "I'd appreciate that."

She handed me a bag, and picked up another one herself. Then we carried them into the house and set them down on the kitchen counter.

When we went back for a second load, Stephanie made her move. While Mrs. Beekman leaned into the car, I stood right behind her, and waved over at the hedge. Out of the corner of my eye, I saw a red blob shoot across the yard, up the steps, and into the house. Then Mrs. Beekman turned around and handed me more groceries.

"Whew!" I said without thinking.

"Too heavy?" Mrs. Beekman asked.

"Oh. No. Just fine. No problem. Perfect." I said. I knew I was babbling a little, but I couldn't help it. Stephanie was safely inside!

Mrs. Beekman and I left the second load of groceries on the counter, and made one more trip to the car and back.

"Thank you very much, Lauren," Mrs. Beekman said after we'd set down the last bags. "How about a cup of hot chocolate?"

"That would be great," I said. I figured I'd better

hang around. After all, Stephanie still had to get *out* of the Beekmans' house.

And as if to remind me that we weren't home free yet, there was a loud thump overhead. It was coming from Kate's room! Mrs. Beekman saw me look nervously up at the ceiling.

"It's only Fredericka," she said with a smile. Fredericka is Kate's kitten, sister to my Rocky, Stephanie's Cinders, and Patti's Adelaide. "I'm constantly amazed by how much noise a five-pound cat can make."

More like an eighty pound girl, I said to myself.

Mrs. Beekman took two cups out of the cabinet. She poured cocoa into them, then added milk, threw in a couple of marshmallows, and popped them into the microwave. "Cookies?" she said to me.

"Sure," I said. Besides wanting to give Stephanie as much time as possible, I was actually feeling pretty hungry. Being nervous pumps up my appetite. Kate and Stephanie tease me about having a hollow leg, but I think it's just that I'm still a growing girl.

I took off my jacket, Mrs. Beekman pulled the cups of chocolate out of the microwave. Then she and I sat down at the kitchen table. She asked me how I was doing on my own in the afternoon, and how my mom's job at Sawyer Insurance was going.

"Fine," I said. Then I ate three almond cookies in a row — almond cookies are pretty small, after all — and asked Mrs. Beekman what was new at the hospital. She's a volunteer at Central County Hospital, where Dr. Beekman works.

I was reaching for a fourth cookie — Kate's parents are both terrific cooks and those almond cookies were really excellent — when there was a loud click and a thud from the front hall.

"I think that was the front door," Mrs. Beekman said, peering over my shoulder. "Melissa, is that you?" she called out.

"I'll take a look," I said quickly, scrambling to my feet.

I walked into the hall. It was empty. I looked up the stairs. No sign of Stephanie. Then I opened the front door just in time to see a flash of red disappearing down the sidewalk. We'd actually pulled it off!

I walked back into the kitchen. "There's nobody there," I told Mrs. Beekman. "It must have been the wind against the door or something." I picked up my jacket. "I guess I'd better get home now," I said. It was almost four-thirty, and I really didn't want Kate

47

to catch me at her house. "I'm supposed to be setting the table. Thanks for the cookies."

"And thank *you* for your help," Mrs. Beekman said.

When I got home, Stephanie was waiting for me in my backyard. "I did it!" she squealed. Stephanie was practically jumping up and down with excitement. She opened her jacket and took out Kate's old plant A — it looked a little squashed — and waved it around. "I should be a spy!"

"You didn't do it alone, you know!" I said crossly. I was actually feeling pretty guilty about fooling Mrs. Beekman. She's a nice lady, *and* she makes fantastic cookies.

"You were great!" said Stephanie. "You did everything just right. Keeping Mrs. B. talking like that so I could get down the stairs and out the front door. What a team!"

When I didn't say anything, Stephanie added in a quieter voice, "Come on, Lauren. Kate's absolutely going to flip her lid when she checks out plant A! She's never going to be Miss Logical again!"

The idea of Kate actually having a thought that wasn't totally sensible cheered me up right away.

"You think?" I said.

48

Stephanie nodded. "Definitely." Then we both grinned.

"Well, I guess I better shove off," Stephanie said. "Here," she said, handing me the plant. "Maybe your mother can save this one."

"Yeah," I agreed. "I'd better get started on my chores."

"Good work, pal!" Stephanie said, giving me a high five. "See you tomorrow."

Then she got on her bike and rode off.

I'd just finished setting the table for dinner when the telephone rang.

"Hello, Lauren?" Stephanie sounded worried. "I've lost the pin!"

"What pin?" I asked.

"My mom's pin! The rhinestone lightning bolt that was on my red jacket!"

"Oh, no! Where?" I said.

"*You* tell *me*," Stephanie groaned. "At your house, in your backyard, in the alley, in Donald's hedge, in Donald's yard. . . ."

"In Kate's hedge, in Kate's yard, in Kate's house . . . in Kate's *room*. . . ," I finished the list for her.

"Right," Stephanie said glumly.

"I'll take a quick look around," I said, "and call you back."

It was getting dark outside, so I grabbed a flashlight out of the front closet. Then I started retracing our steps.

But this time, unfortunately, Bullwinkle was wide awake. As soon as I got close to the garage, he started barking his head off. And just as I was checking out Donald Foster's hedge, a window flew open downstairs in the Fosters' house.

"What's going on?" It was Donald.

"Just what I needed!" I muttered to myself.

"Hide and seek?" Donald drawled through the window. He likes to think of himself as years older than Kate, Stephanie, Patti, and me and tons more sophisticated.

I swiched off my flashlight. "No," I said. "I've lost something."

"Your mittens," Donald said, brushing his blond hair back. I guess he was referring to the nursery rhyme, which I didn't think was very funny at all.

"No," I snapped. "A valuable rhinestone pin! Would you mind letting me know if you see it?"

Donald stared at me. "Excu-u-use me!" he huffed, slamming the window shut.

Feeling pretty cross, I decided to go back to my house before Bullwinkle alerted the entire neighborhood that something was up.

I quickly dialed Stepahanie's private number.

She answered on the first ring. "Find it?" she asked breathlessly.

"Nope," I said.

"Oh, wow." Stephanie sounded worried. "I hope *Kate* doesn't find it. . . ."

"If she does, we'll know soon enough," I said gloomily. "See you in the morning."

Then we both hung up.

Chapter
7

But when Stephanie, Kate, Patti, and I met on the corner of Pine the next morning, Kate didn't say a thing. She didn't mention the rhinestone pin or plant A, either.

She acted like plain old unsuspecting Kate Beekman all the way to school. She told us about the Video Club meeting the afternoon before. She described how Charlie Garner and Mark Freedman had gotten into this really big argument with Betsy Chalfin and Erin Wilson about whose turn it was to borrow the video camera. Kate said Erin had gotten so mad she called Charlie a "dough-brain." That made Ms. Gilberto so upset she almost wrung her hands off at the wrists. Ms. Gilberto's our art teacher. She hates arguments, but she's usually too timid to stop them.

In fact, the only out-of-the-ordinary thing that happened all day long was when school was over at three. The four of us walked to the bike rack and unlocked our bikes, as always. But instead of pointing herself up Hillcrest with Stephanie, Patti, and me, Kate turned her bike in the opposite direction.

"Aren't you coming with us?" Patti asked.

"No," Kate replied. "I'm going down to Main Street."

"Main Street?" Stephanie repeated.

"There's . . . um . . . some stuff I want to look up in the library," Kate said. "See you guys."

Stephanie waited until she and I had waved good-bye to Patti and turned off on Pine Street. Then she turned to me. "What do you think about Kate?" she demanded. "Do you think she actually didn't *notice* that one of her plants had grown a good inch more than the other?!"

I shrugged my shoulders. "I guess it's *possible*," I said.

"And why's she going to the library today?" Stephanie asked, stopping at the end of my driveway.

53

"Do you think there's a connection?"

I didn't have any idea. All I knew was, the next move was Kate's. It was just a matter of time.

Coincidentally, our sleepover was at Kate's house that week. And it wasn't until we were riding to school that Friday morning that Kate said, "I have something . . . uh . . . kind of amazing to show you guys tonight."

Stephanie groaned. "Kate," she said, "you didn't rent that Russian movie again!" One of Kate's favorite movies of all time is at least fifty years old. It's in black and white, naturally, and it's three-and-a-half hours long, and all the actors speak only Russian!

"No, it's not the Russian movie," Kate said. "Something *really* incredible."

Stephanie and I sneaked a quick glance at each other. It had to be the plant, right? What else could Kate Beekman be thinking that was more incredible than her Russian movie? Stephanie and I were both having a hard time controlling our giggles.

"Can't you give us a hint?" Stephanie asked, clearing her throat and trying to look serious.

"Uh-uh." After that, Kate clammed up completely. No matter how hard we tried, we couldn't get anything else out of her for the rest of the day.

As I was leaving my house that evening, Mrs. Green was just dropping Stephanie off at the Beekmans'. "Stephanie, wait up," I called. We stood on the curb for a second.

"Boy, am I glad I ran into you!" Stephanie whispered. "What should we do when Kate shows us those plants?" She giggled. "Should we yell, 'Gotcha!' right away? Or let Kate go on about them for a while?"

I grinned. "I think we should try to look totally surprised, and let her go on about them!" I said as we started up the walk. "Kate should have plenty of time to experience first-hand what it's like to have a runaway imagination."

"Yeah!" Stephanie nodded.

When we rang the bell, Patti opened the door. "Come on in," she said. "We're just stocking up on snacks in the kitchen."

Kate was busy cutting a pan of her super-fudge into neat, little squares on the kitchen table, while Melissa rooted around in the fridge.

"Hi, guys," Kate said.

"Hi. Where's the big surprise?" I asked innocently.

Kate frowned her "not-around-Melissa" frown. She nodded toward her little sister. "Not here," she said. "Upstairs."

"You can keep your dumb old secrets!" Melissa announced. She stuck her tongue out at her sister. "I'll bet your secrets are as boring as you are! I don't care. Mom, Dad, and I are watching the financial news!" Then she marched off into the living room.

"You know," Stephanie said thoughtfully, "I think it was Melissa they were writing about in Lauren's newspaper. You know, the article about the second-grader who's actually a hundred-year-old alien?"

"Yeah, right, Stephanie," I said. "Dump on me for believing everything I read. I'm tough. I can take it."

Kate gave us an odd look, but she still didn't say anything about her spider plants. Instead, she pried the fudge squares neatly out of the pan with the knife and stacked them on a platter. Then she set the platter on a tray already piled high with blue corn chips, guacamole dip, and Cokes.

Patti, Stephanie, and I grabbed glasses and napkins and plates, and the four of us headed upstairs.

"The suspense is killing me!" Stephanie whispered as we followed Kate and Patti into Kate's bedroom.

"Just keep a straight face!" I whispered back.

Kate set the tray on her rug. Stephanie, Patti, and I put the plates and munchies down next to it.

Then Kate announced solemnly, "You'd better sit down for this."

The three of us lined up on her double bed.

"Yeah?" Stephanie asked.

Kate studied our faces. "Do you all have a good grip on yourselves?" she asked in a low voice.

I rolled my eyes at Stephanie. What a build-up! But where were the plants?

"We're ready," Patti answered.

"Then take a look at this!" Kate walked over to the window and pulled up the blinds.

And there were the two spider plants, side by side on the windowsill.

But Stephanie and I didn't have to fake our surprise — the gasps from both of us were absolutely real!

Plant A was larger than Plant B, all right — about *three* times larger! Plant B was still about two-

and-a-half inches tall, the same size it had been at my house on Saturday. But plant A had grown at least three inches taller!

"Can you believe it?" Kate whispered, looking as shocked as Stephanie, Patti, and I. "I think I've got . . . the *power*!"

Chapter
8

The three of us on the bed were too stunned to say a word.

"I first noticed it on Tuesday," Kate told us. "I came up here before dinner, after I'd gotten home from Video Club, and plant A looked a little larger to me that plant B. So I took my ruler out of the desk drawer and measured. And plant A seemed to have grown a whole inch!"

Stephanie and I glanced at each other. So far, so good. That was the afternoon Stephanie had replaced the *old* plant A with the *new* plant A from Mrs. Talley's, while I'd kept Kate's mom busy in the kitchen. But then Kate's story started to get weird. . . .

"After dinner that night," she went on, "I came upstairs and did what I'd been doing every night since Saturday. I'd leave plant B on the windowsill. But I'd move plant A over to the desk."

Kate picked up the big spider plant, which looked ready to burst out of its pot, and moved it to her desk. Then she sat down on her desk chair. "I'd sit right in front of it on the chair," Kate said. "And then I'd put both hands on the pot, and imagine the white light shining out of my ceiling, flowing into my head and down through my shoulders. . . ."

I nodded and swallowed, hard. Things were getting kind of spooky!

"I'd imagine the warmth flowing out of my hands, through the clay pot, and into the spider plant's roots. . . ."

Kate turned to look at the three of us. "I'd usually only do it for about five minutes because I thought the whole thing was garbage anyway, not to mention a major waste of time. But Tuesday night, after I'd noticed the difference in the size of the plants, I did it for about ten minutes instead. And . . . the very next morning" — Kate lowered her voice almost to a whisper — "plant A was practically four inches tall!"

A chill ran down the back of my neck.

"That afternoon, I went to the public library to look for a book on psychic powers," Kate went on. "And I found one called *Warming Up Your Psychic Skills*."

"Do you have it here?" I asked her.

"No," Kate said. "It's a reserve book, so I couldn't check it out, but I read a few of the chapters. And on Wednesday night I tried out some of the suggestions."

"L-like what?" Stephanie stammered. Patti just stared at the plant, wide-eyed.

"First you have to relax completely," Kate told us. "You take off your shoes, and loosen your clothes if they're at all tight. Then you turn the lights down low." Kate switched off her desk lamp. The only light in the room came from the small pole lamp in the corner. "Turn off the radio, stereo or television so there's no background noise at all. Then sit down in a comfortable chair, or even lie down on your bed."

"Uh-huh," Stephanie and I said. We sure weren't having any trouble keeping a straight face *now*!

"Then let go, beginning with your toes," Kate said. Her voice gave me shivers. It sounded all dreamy and far away, not like the voice of the no-nonsense Kate Beekman I knew.

"Let go?" Patti said in a hushed voice.

"That's right. First you tighten up your toes. Then, very slowly, you relax them totally. You do the same thing with your ankles, your calves, your knees, all the way up your body," said Kate. "You breathe deeply, too — breathing in when you tighten up, and breathing out when you relax."

I slipped off my sneakers and tried it with my toes: tighten, breath in. Loosen, breath out. It seemed easy enough.

"When you get to your head," Kate said, "first, relax your jaw, then your mouth, then your eyes and forehead. Once you've done all that, clear your mind of all your troubles — think of blue sky, fluffy clouds, or calm oceans. *Then* let the white light flow into your head!"

Kate stroked the spider plant's long, thin leaves. "So that's what I did on Wednesday night." She continued in the same dreamy voice: "First I relaxed. Then I imagined the white light for three times as long as usual. I must have spent fifteen minutes or so on it. And by the next morning. . . ." She fixed us with her eyes. ". . . the plant had grown another whole inch!"

"Wow!" Patti shaped the word with her mouth, but no sound went with it.

"After a session of twenty minutes last night," Kate said, "It was *six inches tall*!"

"I'd like to try that relaxing stuff, Kate," Patti said a little shakily. "Scoot over, please, Lauren." She kicked off her shoes and lay down on Kate's bed.

"Me, too." Stephanie pushed the tray and all the food out of the way. Then she stretched out on one side of the rug. I stretched out on the other side.

Kate led us through all the steps so that we'd *really* relax completely. She led us through loosening our toes, our ankles, our knees, up to our necks, jaws, mouths, and eyes.

It took a while — at least ten minutes or so.

"Are you feeling relaxed?" Kate asked when Patti and Stephanie and I had finally finished with our foreheads.

"Yes," the three of us murmured.

"Clear your minds," Kate ordered.

I thought of the ocean on an absolutely still day: the water was a flat, sparkling blue-green, stretching to the horizon in front of me. I was beginning to feel totally loose, almost as if I were floating.

After some time had passed, I heard Kate say, "Now think of the white light!"

I imagined the white light pouring out of the ceiling, bathing me totally in brightness and heat, sinking down into my head, flowing past my shoulders, down my arms, and into my hands. . . .

Kate stepped over to me and held out the spider plant so I could touch it for a minute or two. Next she went to Stephanie, and finally to Patti. Then she set the plant back in the window. "After that dose," she said, "it ought to be eight inches tall by tomorrow morning."

"Have you tried anything else?" Patti asked her.

Kate lowered the blind. "Like what?"

"Oh, like finding something that's lost," Patti replied. "Or getting somebody to call you on the phone."

"No." Kate shook her head. "Just making the plant grow."

"Why don't you try something else now?" Patti said excitedly. "Get someone to call us!"

"Who should I try it on?" Kate asked.

"Why not Kyle again?" I suggested. "We're ninety-nine percent certain he's at home, watching movies on TV, so you know exactly where to beam your thoughts."

"You think I ought to?" Kate looked doubtful. "It's one thing to mess with plants, but I wouldn't want to — "

"Try it!" Stephanie urged.

"Well, okay," Kate agreed at last. "But I'd better lie down."

Patti scrambled off the bed to sit on the desk chair. Stephanie and I stayed where we were, on the rug.

"I can't guarantee anything, though," Kate said, untying her sneakers. "I'll just have to see if *the power* works for stuff like this, too!"

She took off her sneakers and placed them neatly beside her bed. Then she stretched out with her head on a pillow. "Patti, please turn that pole lamp down some more," she said.

Patti jumped up, dimmed the three-way pole lamp, and sat down again.

Then Stephanie, Patti, and I watched Kate relax, starting with her toes. It took some time, and I found myself breathing deeply, in and out, along with Kate. I might even have fallen asleep in the warm, dark room if I hadn't had such butterflies in my stomach.

By the time Kate had gotten to her forehead, the butterflies were really jumping around. Did Kate really have *the power*? Maybe Mrs. Talley had added some secret fertilizer to plant A that was still working. That was probably the answer. Wasn't it?

You could have heard a pin drop in Kate's bedroom. Then she laid her right arm across her eyes and started to hum softly to herself, kind of a creepy little sound, without any tune.

I really *didn't* want the phone to ring, but my ears were straining to hear it if it did. . . .

BRRRRINGGG! The noise was so startling that I almost screamed!

"The phone. . . ," Kate murmured, without moving from her place on the bed.

It rang again, and stopped. About five seconds later, Melissa pounded up the stairs.

"Kate!" she screeched. "It's for you!"

Melissa pushed open the bedroom door and peered inside. "You're sitting in here in the dark? You guys are *weird*!"

Weirder than she knew!

"Who is it, Melissa?" Kate said, her arm still lying across her eyes.

"He said it was Kyle," Melissa replied over her shoulder, and skipped back down the hall.

Chapter 9

"Kyle!" I barely managed to squeak.

"I can't believe it!" Stephanie practically choked.

"You did it, Kate!" Patti added in a voice hardly above a whisper.

Kate slowly sat up on her bed. "That really took it out of me," she murmured. She pushed herself to her feet and kind of teetered through her bedroom door, and out into the hall. We followed her.

Kate picked up the phone. "Hello?" Then she turned the phone around toward us, so we could hear Kyle say, "Hey, Kate — it's Kyle Hubbard."

Kate pressed the phone back to her ear. "Oh. Hi, Kyle. . . . *Beast of Blood?*" Kate said. "That's a classic — what time is it on?"

Kyle was just letting her know about a movie on TV, which he might have done without any hocus-pocus — mightn't he?

". . . Oh, really? . . . Well. Thanks. And thanks for calling." Kate hung up the phone and walked back into her bedroom.

"What did he say?" Patti asked her.

"He said . . . he was just sitting in the den, watching *Friday Chillers*," Kate answered, "when all of a sudden it was like a car alarm went off in his head!"

"A car alarm. . . ," I repeated, and shivered.

"And he felt this tremendous urge to call me. So he figured he'd let me know about *Beast of Blood*, which is on at ten o'clock, and kill two birds with one stone," Kate said.

She flopped down on her bed again. "I am ex-*hausted!*" she said. "I'm also starving!"

"It must take enormous amounts of energy to do what you just did," Patti said understandingly. "What you need is some food!"

Patti dished out some guacamole dip and blue corn chips and poured Kate a big glass of Coke. Kate really dug in. But the rest of us seemed to have lost our appetites, even me.

Suddenly we weren't just the regular Sleepover Friends anymore: some shorter, some taller, some neater, some messier, some smarter, some better at sports. Suddenly there were three regular Sleepover Friends — and one Sleepover Psychic!

Maybe Kate was turning into a mind reader, too, because then she looked straight at the three of us and said, "I hope you guys aren't going to feel funny about this psychic business."

"Absolutely not!" Stephanie replied quickly.

"No way!" I said a little too loudly.

"It'll be really useful," Patti said, trying to be soothing.

"Right, like if we need a boost in the garden next summer," Stephanie said.

"Or maybe some silverware straightened out," I added. Surely anybody who could make plants grow could straighten out spoons that got bent in the dishwasher.

"Or if we lose something. . . ," Patti said.

"I *did* lose something!" Stephanie exclaimed.

"Stephanie!" I muttered through my teeth. Was she actually going to tell Kate about the rhinestone pin?!

"You remember my mom's rhinestone pin?" Stephanie plowed ahead. "The one in the shape of a lightning bolt?"

"Sure." Kate nodded.

"I lost it on Tuesday afternoon. . . ." Stephanie broke off.

"Where were you?" Kate asked.

"Uh . . . uh . . . somewhere around Lauren's house, I think," Stephanie fumbled. "It fell off my red jacket, and I *have* to find it — my mom is ready to kill me. It was one of her favorite pins. Do you think you could figure out where it is?"

"I don't know," Kate replied slowly. "In *Psychic Skills* there were people who found lost dogs, and lost kids, and even lost gold mines, so I suppose. . . ."

"Why don't you try it, Kate?" Patti said.

"All right. Give me a second to relax myself." Kate set her plate and glass on the floor and lay back down on the bed. Then she closed her eyes and breathed deeply for a couple of minutes. "I'm thinking about the rhinestone pin. . . ," she said in that new spooky voice of hers.

Patti, Stephanie, and I sat stock-still and waited for her to go on.

"I see it on Stephanie's red down jacket," Kate murmured. "Now it's . . . coming unhooked. It's barely hanging on. I see lots of . . . sticks . . . branches! The pin's getting caught on a branch . . . it's getting snatched off her jacket!"

All the hairs on the back of my neck were standing up!

"The pin is falling. . . ," Kate went on. "The pin is falling off the red jacket . . . I see it falling into . . . into brown leaves . . . dead leaves. The dead leaves are piled up around the bottoms of bushes. . . ."

"The hedges!" Stephanie hissed to me. "Definitely the hedges. The pin must have fallen off when we crawled through them on Tuesday!"

"Which one?" I whispered back, staring at Kate's face. Her eyes were shut tight. Was the pin in the hedge between my house and the Fosters', or in Kate's hedge? I hoped it hadn't gotten lost in *Kate's* hedge, like when Stephanie's hair had gotten caught on that branch. We'd never be able to explain what we were doing lurking around outside the Beekmans'. . . .

"I hear a . . . a dog barking," Kate went on in a low voice.

Had Kate read my mind again?!

"I think it's Bullwinkle barking . . . I think the pin is in the hedge between Lauren's and the Fosters'!"

"This is incredible!" Stephanie sounded as if she were about to faint. I could understand how she felt. I was feeling pretty strange myself.

Kate sat up and rubbed her eyes. "Is that possible?" she asked Stephanie and me. "About the pin?"

"Definitely," Stephanie said. "We were — "

"We were fooling around with Bullwinkle," I interrupted quickly, "and that's probably when it fell off."

"Yeah, fooling around with Bullwinkle," Stephanie repeated. "You're a lifesaver, Kate. I was beginning to think my mom would never forgive me for losing that pin." Stephanie scrambled up off the floor. "Let's go look for it right now."

"My parents wouldn't exactly be wild about us

wandering around outside at this time of night," Kate said, pointing to her clock-radio. It was ten-fifteen. "We'll look for it in the morning."

"No, let's wait till they've gone to bed, and then go out, okay, Kate?" Stephanie said. "Please? I'm dying to know if you're right. The pin might start to rust if it stays outdoors much longer. . . ."

Stephanie looked so anxious that Kate gave in. "All right. I guess we can," she said. Then she turned on the portable TV, which was in her room for the evening. "In the meantime," she said with a grin, "let's check out *Beast of Blood*!" Some things will never change with Kate, thank goodness.

I usually argue about not wanting to watch scary movies, especially *gory* scary movies. With my imagination, I usually end up having nightmares for weeks. But with all this psychic stuff going on in *real life*, the *Beast of Blood* hardly fazed me at all. He looked pretty tame next to my own best friend, the Great Kate, our personal Sleepover Psychic!

When *Beast of Blood* finally ended at eleven-thirty, all four of us sneaked downstairs and slipped out the Beekmans' kitchen door.

74

"Boy, is it dark out here!" Stephanie whispered as we stepped off the back steps.

"That's because it's night!" Kate muttered.

"That's because there's no moon," Stephanie corrected her. "Why don't you turn on the flashlight?" Kate had brought along her mini-light.

"Sure," Kate snapped. "So my parents can glance out their bedroom window, decide that we're burglars, and call the police? I'll turn it on when we get to Lauren's fence." It was a flash of the old sensible Kate I already found myself missing like crazy.

"Yipes!" Patti squeaked. "Watch out for the swing. It just reaches out and grabs you!"

Despite how dark it was, we managed to stumble to the first hedge. We squeezed through it, and the four of us crept across Donald's backyard to the second hedge, the one between his house and mine.

"Where do we look?" Stephanie asked in a low voice. There were plenty of lilac bushes to choose from, since the hedge is about thirty feet long.

Kate put her hand over her eyes and concentrated. "I have a strong feeling the pin's in the bushes closest to the back alley," she said at last.

Stephanie nudged me with her elbow. "Amazing!" she whispered. The spot Kate pointed to was exactly where Stephanie and I had pushed through the hedge on Tuesday afternoon!

Kate switched on the mini-light, and the four of us started crawling on our hands and knees in and out of the bare lilac stems and dead leaves. I was thinking a lot about Kate's strange powers, and a little about the *Beast of Blood*, when suddenly I heard a creaking noise. . . .

All four of us froze.

But before we could get too panicky, Donald Foster drawled from his window, "What's wrong with you guys? Have you already lost something else?"

"Uh-oh," Stephanie muttered.

"Sssh!" Kate switched off the light.

"Go away, Donald!" I hissed. All Stephanie and I needed was for him to bring up the pin!

Which is exactly what Donald did, not three seconds later. "You can't be looking for the pin," he said. "Kate told me you'd found it. So what are you . . ."

"Kate told you wha-at?!" Stephanie and I shrieked at the same time.

"GOTCHA!" shouted Kate, and she and Patti burst out laughing.

Right at that moment Bullwinkle started barking like crazy on the other side of the hedge. I think the four of us covered the half-block from where we were to Kate's back steps in about twenty seconds flat!

We thundered through the Beekmans' kitchen door, slammed it shut, and locked it tight.

"Girls, is everything all right down there?" Mrs. Beekman called from upstairs.

"Just fine, Mom," Kate called back, still giggling.

"Until Lauren and I get our hands on you!" Stephanie said to Kate. She pretended she was going to grab Kate's neck and give it a good squeeze!

"The plant. The pin. They were faked?!" I yelped. "Even Kyle?"

"Sure. I just asked Kyle to call me around nine-thirty," Kate said smugly.

"What a rotten trick, Kate!" I said. "I really believed you had psychic powers!" I was pretty steamed up — I felt like a total jerk for being taken in so easily.

"You guys started it, with that Jack-in-the-beanstalk spider-plant routine," Kate sniffed. "More fairy-tales!"

"When did you figure it out?" Stephanie asked her.

"On Tuesday, I found the rhinestone pin on the stairs, so I knew Stephanie'd been in the house," Kate said. "My mom finally admitted you'd stopped by, Lauren. But she said she hadn't seen Stephanie at all. She also said *you'd* never left the kitchen. Which made it pretty clear that you guys had been up to something. When I saw that plant A had grown an inch since that morning, I was sure that one of you'd snuck in my room and replaced it. What other explanation could there possibly be?"

No other explanation, not for good, old Kate. Usually I would have found the sensible way she'd seen through our plan pretty annoying, but I realized I was too relieved to have the Kate I knew back again. I felt a lot more comfortable with old 'mind over matter,' logical-to-a-fault Kate, than with O Great Kate, the Sleepover Psychic.

"So Patti and I bought an even bigger spider plant on Thursday," Kate went on.

"You were in on this, too?" Stephanie asked Patti. She blushed and nodded.

"Sure," Kate said with a glance at Stephanie. "I *knew* Patti was innocent — she'd been helping her dad the day you and Lauren did the dirty deed. Besides," she went on sternly, "Patti had to have *some* fun. You guys were *ruining* her psychic experiment."

"Where'd you buy the plant?" I asked.

"At Hearts and Flowers, where else?" Kate said. "You told us you'd been there, sending a rose to Linda." She paused and then she giggled. "I'm just sorry Donald Foster butted in," she said. "I was going to stick the pin in the hedge, and then make a big deal about uncovering it with my new-found powers. You guys would have been completely convinced!" Kate reached into her pocket, and handed the rhinestone pin back to Stephanie. "And then," she added, "I had an even bigger surprise planned for you tomorrow."

"Like what?" Stephanie asked. "Replacing the spider plant with one big enough to eat Riverhurst?" I could tell Stephanie was still a little peeved that Kate had seen through our trick.

"No. I've used my powerful brain waves on Roger and Linda," Kate said solemnly. "And I predict that, by four o'clock tomorrow afternoon, they'll be back together."

"Sure, and UFO's landed in Wisconsin," I said.

"Loosen up, Lauren. You have to have the right attitude or this psychic stuff doesn't have a chance of working!" Kate said. Then she cracked up.

Chapter
10

And that was how Kate, Patti, Stephanie, and I ended up sitting on a bench on the north side of the mall at about three-forty-five on Saturday afternoon. We'd brought along some chocolate-covered cherries from Sweet Stuff to give us something to do.

"So — what are we supposed to be looking at?" Stephanie said. "The towel shop? The swimming pool store, which is closed for the winter? The back doors of Gallo's Twin Cinemas?" she sniffed. "Not too lively, is it?"

It *is* pretty deserted around there, especially if Gallo's Twin Cinemas are both running their movies, like they were then.

"Cool it," Kate said. She got comfortable and

dug into the bag of candy. "You'll see soon enough."

"This better not be a joke!" muttered Stephanie with a suspicious glance in Kate's direction.

Not three minutes later, the door of one of the Twin Cinemas pushed open, and people started to stream out.

Kate sat up straight to stare at the crowd. "Now we're coming to it!" she murmured. "The last amazing act of O Great Kate before she goes into early retirement!"

We saw a bunch of kids from Riverhurst High coming out of the cinema. Tug Keeler was there *without* Barbara Baxter, some kids from Junior High. . . . Todd Schwartz, with Mary Beth Young, and . . .

"It's Al Frances!" Stephanie cried.

"Al Frances!" Kate scowled. "He's not supposed to be. . . ."

"It's okay," Patti said. "He's with Janet Ahrens."

Janet Ahrens, Roger's conceited, snobby old girlfriend, was walking alongside Al. She was looking up at him adoringly — she'd never treated Roger like that!

As Al and Janet headed out the side door of the mall, I turned to Kate, "Was this the big surprise?"

Kate was still scanning the movie crowd, which was beginning to thin out.

"There they are!" she cried at last. "Behind the guy wearing a green cap!"

The man bent over to tie his shoe, and then I saw them, too. "Roger and Linda!" I exclaimed. "Together!"

They were strolling slowly along, holding hands. Linda was beaming up at my brother, and my brother was gazing down at her with this really embarrassing sappy grin on his face. While we watched, Roger leaned over and kissed the tip of Linda's nose before they wandered up the main aisle of the mall.

"Wooo!" Stephanie said. "Way to go! Love is wonderful, isn't it?" She raised an eyebrow. "It makes you deaf, dumb, and blind, too. They looked right at this bench, and they didn't even see us!"

"I definitely owe you one, Kate," I said. "How did you do it?"

Kate covered her eyes with her hand. "First I tightened my toes . . . then I loosened them, breathing slowly in, and out. . . ."

Stephanie gave Kate's right arm a good smack, and I smacked the other arm myself. "Come on!" I said. "The rose didn't work, the candy didn't work, what *did* work?"

"Heavy psychic powers," Kate began. But when I started to punch her again, she giggled and said, "And two tickets to the movie of last year's Heat concert tour."

"Oh, is it playing *here*?" Stephanie said. There was no way to tell, since we were facing the back door of Cinema II.

Kate nodded. "And you said Heat was their favorite group, Lauren, so I sent Linda a ticket signed 'R,' and Roger a ticket signed 'L,' and hoped for the best. You owe me eight dollars."

It was a lot of money, but it was worth it! Roger and Linda were back to normal, and O Great Kate was back to normal, too. And I was *definitely* back to normal. . . . I was suddenly hungry enough to eat my way across the mall.

"How about a double-cheese pizza at the Pizza Palace? My stomach feels totally empty," I said. "And then maybe ice-cream bars at Frozen Delights . . . and . . ."

The four of us headed toward the middle of the mall, and civilization. I couldn't wait to get that double cheese pizza! "I've learned one thing from all this," I told Stephanie, Patti, and Kate as we hurried along.

"What's that?" they said.

"Some things should always stay the same," I said. "Like the Sleepover Friends!"

"Positively," Stephanie agreed.

"Definitely," Kate and Patti chimed in.

Just plain old Sleepover Friends forever!

#20 Lauren in the Middle

I thought Ginger looked a little uneasy as we listened to Kate and Stephanie and Patti come running up the stairs. I couldn't really blame her. After all, she was about to meet three more new people.

Stephanie was the first to burst through the door. Ginger held out her hand, but before Stephanie could shake it, Kate came rushing into the room. "Virginia?" she announced. "I'm Kate Beekman."

"Ginger," I mumbled.

But Kate was running on, "Listen, Lauren, I have to turn on the TV for a minute. . . ."

Meanwhile, Stephanie started checking out her hair in the mirror. "Why is it that as soon as it gets the teeniest bit damp outside," she wailed, "my head looks like it belongs on the bride of Frankenstein?!"

Ginger looked a little lost, but fortunately at that moment Patti spoke to her. "Hi, Ginger—I'm Patti Jenkins. When did you get to Riverhurst?" Good old Patti. At least *she* could be counted on to make polite conversation. It was getting to the point where I was more worried that Ginger wouldn't like Kate and Stephanie, than the other way around.

WIN GIRL TALK DATE LINE –
AN AUDIO DATING GAME!

Enter the

SLEEPOVER™ FRIENDS

Date Line Giveaway!

100 Winners!

It's new! It's exciting! And you can win one! It's GIRL TALK DATE LINE ™ — the game of make-believe and fun! Play it at your next sleepover! Listen to the recorded phone calls and match up boys and girls for dates! Just fill in the coupon below and return by March 1, 1990.

SLEEPOVER FRIENDS Date Line Giveaway

Name _____ Age _____

Street _____

City _____ State _____ Zip _____

Where did you buy this Sleepover Friends book?
☐ Bookstore ☐ Drug Store ☐ Supermarket ☐ Discount Store
☐ Book Club ☐ Book Fair ☐ Other (specify) _____

SLE689

Pack your bags for fun and adventure with

SLEEPOVER FRIENDS™

by Susan Saunders

Join Kate, Lauren, Stephanie and Patti at their great sleepover parties every weekend. Truth or Dare, scary movies, late-night boy talk—it's all part of **Sleepover Friends!**

☐	MF40641-8	**#1 Patti's Luck**	**$2.50**
☐	MF40642-6	**#2 Starring Stephanie**	**$2.50**
☐	MF40643-4	**#3 Kate's Surprise**	**$2.50**
☐	MF40644-2	**#4 Patti's New Look**	**$2.50**
☐	MF41336-8	**#5 Lauren's Big Mix-Up**	**$2.50**
☐	MF41337-6	**#6 Kate's Camp-Out**	**$2.50**
☐	MF41694-4	**#7 Stephanie Strikes Back**	**$2.50**
☐	MF41695-2	**#8 Lauren's Treasure**	**$2.50**
☐	MF41696-0	**#9 No More Sleepovers, Patti?**	**$2.50**
☐	MF41697-9	**#10 Lauren's Sleepover Exchange**	**$2.50**
☐	MF41845-9	**#11 Stephanie's Family Secret**	**$2.50**
☐	MF41846-7	**#12 Kate's Sleepover Disaster**	**$2.50**
☐	MF42301-0	**#13 Patti's Secret Wish**	**$2.50**
☐	MF42300-2	**#14 Lauren Takes Charge**	**$2.50**
☐	MF42299-5	**#15 Stephanie's Big Story**	**$2.50**
☐	MF42662-1	**Sleepover Friends' Super Guide**	**$2.50**
☐	MF42366-5	**#16 Kate's Crush**	**$2.50**
☐	MF42367-3	**#17 Patti Gets Even**	**$2.50**

Available wherever you buy books...or use the coupon below.

Scholastic Inc. P.O. Box 7502, 2932 E. McCarty Street, Jefferson City, MO 65102

Please send me the books I have checked above. I am enclosing $_____

(Please add $1.00 to cover shipping and handling). Send check or money order–no cash or C.O.D.'s please

Name _____

Address _____

City _____ State/Zip _____

Please allow four to six weeks for delivery. Offer good in U.S.A. only. Sorry, mail order not available to residents of Canada. Prices subject to change.

SLE 289

America's Favorite Series

THE BABY-SITTERS CLUB®

by Ann M. Martin

Collect Them All!

The seven girls at Stoneybrook Middle School get into all kinds of adventures...with school, boys, and, of course, baby-sitting!